P9-CQO-348

Sometimes I Feel Like a Mouse

Sometimes I Feel Like a Mouse

A BOOK ABOUT FEELINGS

by Jeanne Modesitt

Illustrated by Robin Spowart

SCHOLASTIC INC. · *New York Toronto London Auckland Sydney*

No part of this publication may be reproduced in whole or in part, or stored
in a retrieval system, or transmitted in any form or by any means, electronic,
mechanical, photocopying, recording, or otherwise, without written
permission of the publisher. For information regarding permission, write to
Scholastic Inc., 730 Broadway, New York, NY 10003.

ISBN 0-590-44836-6

Text copyright © 1992 by Jeanne Modesitt.
Illustrations copyright © 1992 by Robin Spowart.
All rights reserved. Published by Scholastic Inc.

12 11 10 9 8 7 6 5 4 3 2   6 7/9

Printed in the U.S.A.   08

To a very
wonderful person —
YOU!

Sometimes
I feel like
a mouse
hiding
shy

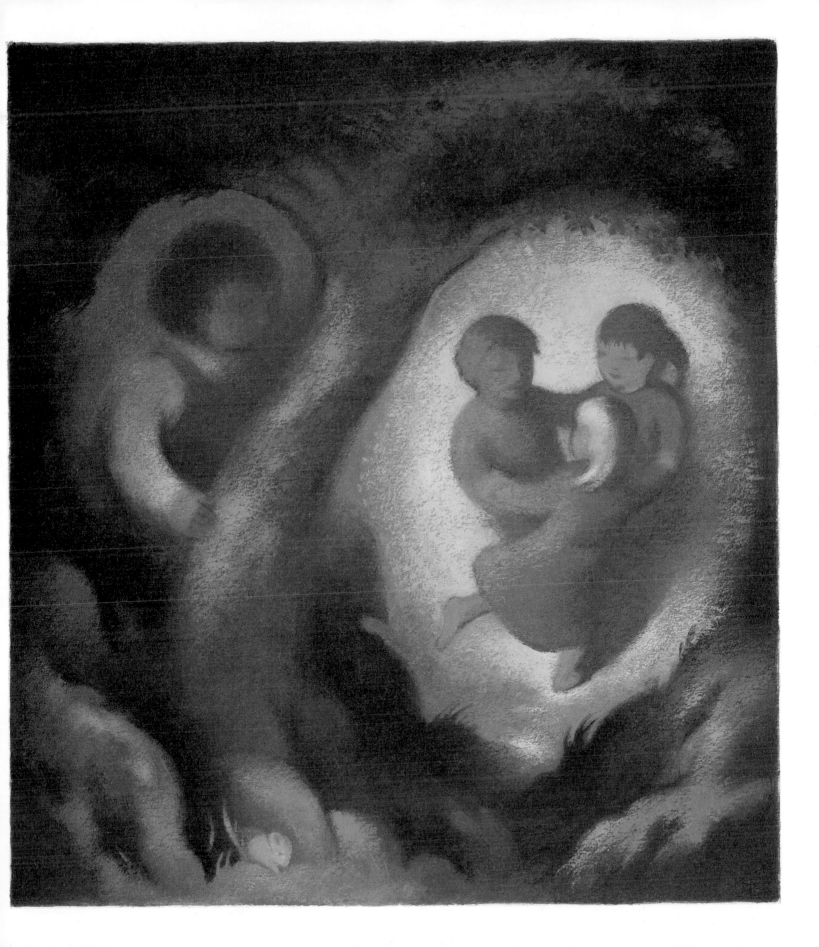

Sometimes
I feel like
an elephant
stomping
bold

Sometimes
I feel like
a wolf
crying
sad

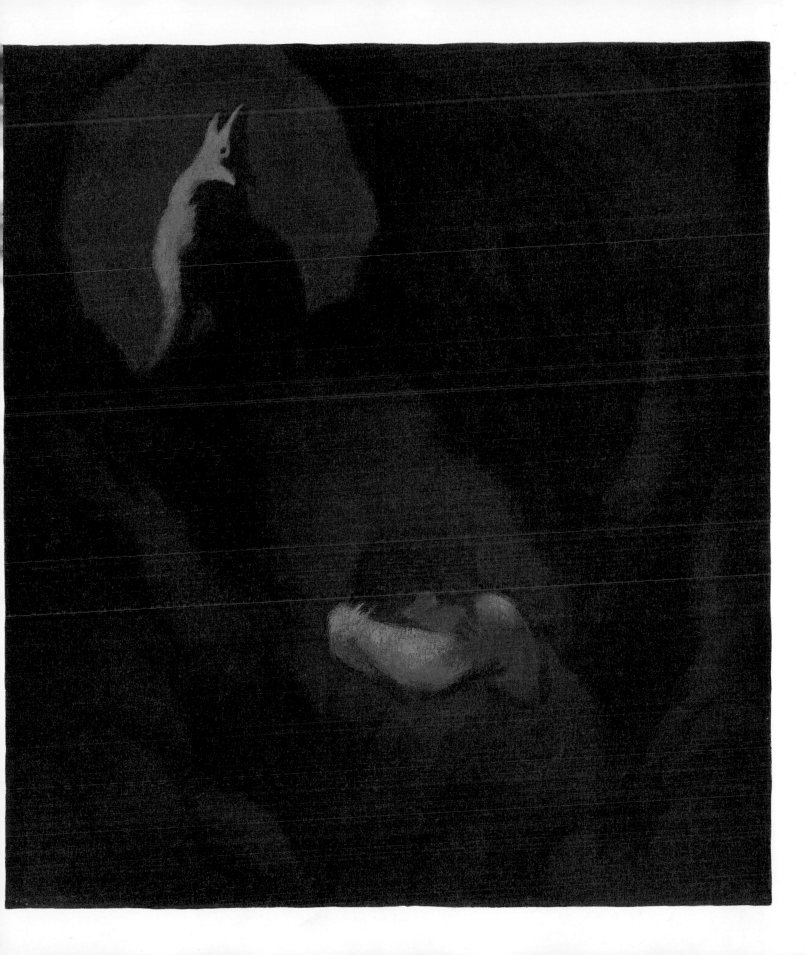

Sometimes
I feel like
a canary
singing
happy

Sometimes
I feel like
a rabbit
trembling
scared

Sometimes
I feel like
a horse
galloping
brave

Sometimes
I feel like
a squirrel
skittering
excited

Sometimes
I feel like
a swan
floating
calm

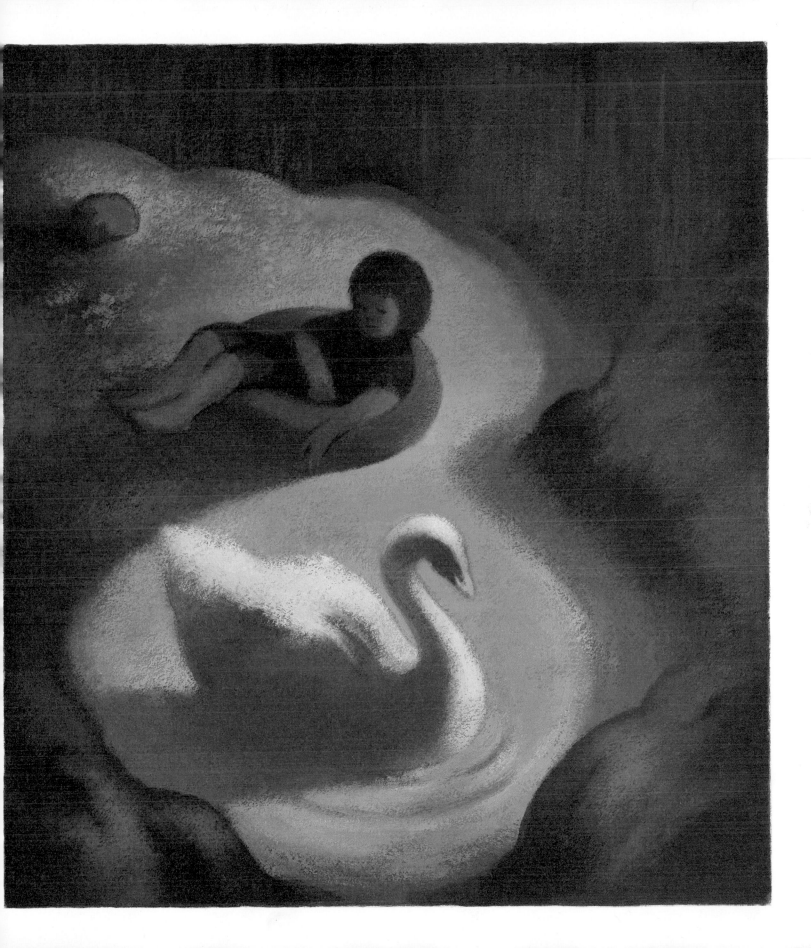

Sometimes
I feel like
a lion
roaring
mad

Sometimes

I feel like

a cat

snuggling

warm

Sometimes
I feel like
a dog
drooping
ashamed

Sometimes
I feel like
an eagle
soaring
proud

Shy,   bold,   sad,

happy,   scared,   brave,

excited,   calm,   mad,

warm,   ashamed,   proud.

I have lots of feelings.
It's wonderful to be me!

About Feelings

Everyone has feelings.

There is no such thing

as a right or a wrong feeling.

All feelings are okay.

Your feelings are your friends.

It's important to listen to them.

What kinds of feelings

did you have today?